Bolton
Council

D1312851

Please return/ renew this item
by the last date shown.
Books can also be renewed at
www.bolton.gov.uk/libraries

As always, for
Colin, Mirren and
Gowan — L. D.

For Reuben,
love from Auntie
Mels x — M. W.

Barefoot Books
2067 Massachusetts Ave
Cambridge, MA 02140

Barefoot Books
29/30 Fitzroy Square
London, W1T 6LQ

Series Editor: Gina Nuttall
Text copyright © 2012 by Lari Don
Illustrations copyright © 2012 by Melanie Williamson
The moral rights of Lari Don and
Melanie Williamson have been asserted

First published in the United States of America by Barefoot Books, Inc
and in Great Britain by Barefoot Books, Ltd in 2012
This paperback edition first published in 2019
All rights reserved

Graphic design by Helen Chapman, West Yorkshire, UK
Cover design by Penny Lamprell, Hampshire, UK
Reproduction by B&P International, Hong Kong
Printed in China on 100% acid-free paper
This book was typeset in Bembo Infant, Cafeteria and Mr. Anteater
The illustrations were prepared in acrylic, pencil and chalk

Thank you to Year 2 at St Anne's Catholic Primary School, Caversham, UK
for all their careful reading

Sources:
Umansky, Kaye. *Three Singing Pigs:
Making Music with Traditional Stories.* A & C Black, London, 2005.

ISBN 978-1-78285-841-6

British Cataloguing-in-Publication Data:
a catalogue record for this book is available from the British Library

Library of Congress Cataloging-in-Publication Data
is available under LCCN 2011032859

1 3 5 7 9 8 6 4 2

The Tortoise's Gift

A Tale from Zambia

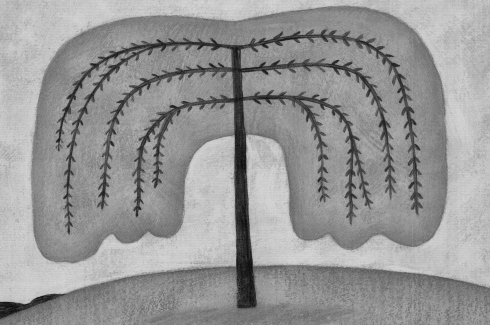

Retold by **Lari Don**   Illustrated by **Melanie Williamson**

Barefoot Books
step inside a story

Contents

CHAPTER 1

The Wonderful Tree

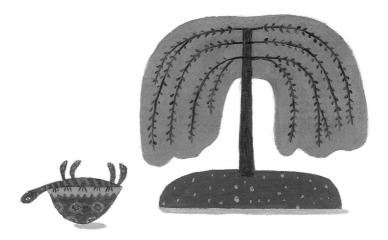

One hot, dry summer in Zambia, the rain stopped falling. Soon the rivers stopped flowing and the grass stopped growing. Soon the animals were very thirsty and very hungry.

The old rabbit had heard stories about a wonderful tree in the middle of the forest. He told the other animals, "When the rain stops falling, this wonderful tree grows every type of delicious fruit. So no animal is ever hungry or thirsty."

The animals searched the middle of the forest and found a strange tree. It was not a palm tree or a baobab tree or a banana tree. The animals did not know what kind of tree it was. So they thought it must be the wonderful tree.

I'm so hungry.

But it looked old and tired and thirsty, just like all the other trees in the forest. It looked like it would not wake up and grow anything until the rains came back.

"There isn't any fruit on it," said
the elephant.

"Maybe we have to tell it what
type of fruit we like," said the chimps.

So they all shouted loudly: "Give
me bananas!", "I want grapes!", "Give
me mangoes!", "I want pineapple!"

But the tree did not grow any
fruit. The lion said, "Maybe there's
a magic word."

"I know what the magic word is,"
squeaked a baby monkey. "Mama says
the magic word is 'please'."

So they all shouted:
"Bananas, please!"
"Mangoes, please!"
But the tree did not
grow any fruit.

"Maybe it doesn't know we're talking to it," said the monkey's mother. "Maybe it thinks we're asking the banana trees for bananas and the mango trees for mangoes."

"So let's call it by its name," suggested the chimps.

"Good idea," said the elephant. "What is its name?"

What is the Tree's Name?

Um . . .

No one knew the tree's name. No one had needed the tree for a long, long time. So now, no one could remember its name.

"Who is old enough to remember the tree's name?" wondered the animals.

14

"What about the mountain?"
said the chimps.

They all looked up and saw the
mountain beyond the forest. It was
pointing up to the sky.

"The mountain has been here
longer than the grass or the trees.
The mountain will know!" they all
agreed.

15

But the mountain was on the other side of the grasslands. It was far away and the animals were all tired and thirsty and hungry.

"Who will go and ask the mountain?" they all wondered.

The lion stepped forward. He said, "I will go! I am the bravest, so I will go. But I want the first pick of the fruit when I bring back the name."

The other animals agreed that was fair.

Me!

So the lion crossed the grasslands
in his quiet, creeping way.

He reached the foot of the huge,
rocky mountain and looked up.

"Mountain, can you please tell
me the name of the wonderful tree
in the middle of the forest?" he asked.

The mountain rumbled,
"AWONGALEMA."

The lion bowed. He said, "Thank you," and he started back across the grasslands.

The lion was very pleased with himself. What a famous hero he would be!

I'm so brave!

He would bring back the name of the tree. Then he would wake up the tree and feed all the animals!

He reached the big red rock halfway across the grasslands. He was so pleased with himself that he decided to stop for a nice big...

Roar!

He stood in the shadow of the rock,
roaring his loudest. And he roared the
name right out of his head!

The lion went slowly back to the
other animals. They were waiting in
a hungry circle around the tree.

The animals asked, "So, what is
the name? Did the mountain tell
you? What is the tree's name?"
The lion was embarrassed. Very
quietly, he said, "I forgot..."

Who Will Try Next?

The animals wondered who else could go to the mountain. Who else could bring the name all the way back?

The elephant stepped forward.
He said, "I will go. I am the biggest,
so I will go."

The other animals thought that
was a very good idea. The elephant
had a very big head, with lots of
space to remember the name.

They agreed that, if the elephant
brought the name back, he could
have first pick of the fruit.

So the elephant crossed the
grasslands in his loud, stomping way.

He reached the foot of the huge,
rocky mountain, and looked up.

"Mountain, please tell me the name
of the wonderful tree in the middle of
the forest?" he asked.

The mountain rumbled,
"AWONGALEMA."

The elephant raised his trunk in
salute. He said, "Thank you," and he
started back across the grasslands.

The elephant was very pleased
with himself. What a famous hero
he would be!

He would bring back the name
of the tree. Then he would wake up
the tree and feed all the animals!

He reached the big red rock
halfway across the grasslands. He
was so pleased with himself that he
decided to stop for a nice, long…

Scratch!

He rubbed his wrinkly hide up against the rock. And he scratched the name right out of his head!

The elephant went slowly back
to the other animals. They were
waiting in a hungry circle around
the tree. The animals asked, "So,
what's the name? Did the mountain
tell you? Can you remember the
tree's name?"

The elephant was embarrassed.
Very quietly, he said, "I forgot…"

CHAPTER 4

The Playful Chimps

The animals wondered who else
could go to the mountain. Who else
could get the name and remember
it and bring it all the way back?

The chimps jumped up and
down. They said, "We will go. We
are the cleverest, so we will go."

The other animals thought that
was a very good idea. After all, the
chimps were very clever. They used
tools and they chattered all the time.
They were so clever that they would
certainly remember the name.

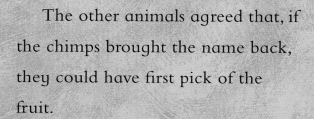

The other animals agreed that, if the chimps brought the name back, they could have first pick of the fruit.

So the chimps crossed the grasslands in their bouncy, chattering way.

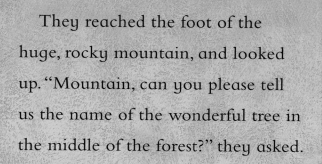

They reached the foot of the huge, rocky mountain, and looked up. "Mountain, can you please tell us the name of the wonderful tree in the middle of the forest?" they asked.

The mountain rumbled, "AWONGALEMA."

The chimps clapped their hands. They said, "Thank you," and they started back across the grasslands. The chimps were very pleased with themselves. What famous heroes they would be!

Hooray! Hooray!

They would bring back the
name of the tree. Then they would
wake up the tree and feed all the
animals!

They reached the big red rock
halfway across the grasslands. They
were so pleased with themselves
that they decided to stop and have
some…

Fun!

They jumped off the rock and
they tickled each other. And they
tickled the name right out of their
heads!

The chimps went slowly back to the forest. The other animals were waiting in a hungry circle around the tree. The animals asked, "So what's the name? Did you listen carefully? What is the tree's name?"

The chimps were embarrassed. Very quietly, they said, "We forgot…"

Sorry.

CHAPTER 5

Slow and Steady

The animals stood hungry and thirsty around the wonderful tree. It still had not fed them. They wondered who could bring back the name now.

A little voice said, "I will go."

The animals looked up and they looked around, but they could not see who had spoken.

The voice said again, "I will go." So the animals looked down. It was the tortoise.

"You can't go," said the animals. "You are too small and you are far too slow. You won't get the name and, even if you do, you'll never bring it back."

But the tortoise said, "I will go." And he did. He crossed the grasslands in his slow, steady way, one step at a time.

Finally, he reached the foot
of the huge, rocky mountain, and
looked up. "Excuse me, Mountain,
can you please tell me the name of
the wonderful tree in the middle of
the forest?" he asked.

Thank you.

The mountain rumbled,
"AWONGALEMA."
The tortoise said, "Awongalema.
Is that right?"
The mountain smiled and
nodded.

40

So the tortoise thanked the mountain and started back across the grasslands. He went slowly and steadily one step at a time.

As he stepped, he chanted, "A – WON – GA – LE – MA."

The tortoise did not feel pleased with himself. The tortoise did not hope he would be famous. He just said, "A – WON – GA – LE – MA."

The tortoise did not stop at the
big red rock. He did not roar or
scratch or tickle. He just kept going,
slowly and steadily, one clawed foot
at a time, saying:

"A – WON – GA – LE – MA."

The tortoise finally reached the
hungry circle of animals around the
tree. He looked up at the tree and
said, "Awongalema, will you please
wake up and feed us all?"

The tree shivered and its
branches creaked. Its tiny leaves
grew wide and green. Its little hard
buds blossomed into big, bright
flowers. As the animals watched, the
petals fell.

44

The flowers swelled and grew
into all sorts of delicious fruit:
bananas, grapes, mangoes and
pineapples! Once the fruit had
ripened for a moment in the sun,
it fell gently to the dry ground.

Every animal in the circle waited
politely for the tortoise to step
forward. Slowly, steadily, one clawed
foot at a time, the tortoise walked
towards the fruit he liked best.

He opened his mouth wide and
took the first bite. It was the most
delicious, the most refreshing,
the juiciest…

...red grape he had ever eaten! The tortoise ate the whole bunch, slowly and steadily, one red grape at a time.

Yum!